A
Tiny
Little Door

poems and illustrations by

Judith Dorian

ISBN: 1461011469
ISBN-13: 9781461011460

Noodle Eater

I like noodles made with butter
I like noodles tossed with cheese
When I eat them with black pepper
I at once begin to sneeze.

Noodles are a funny word
They make a funny runny rhyme
Poodle, doodle and caboodle
Yet the taste of them's sublime.

I like chicken with potatoes
I like chicken from the grill
If I eat some with tomatoes
Then I season it with dill.

To this dish I add egg noodles
Round ones, square ones, short or long
Huge or mini, fat or skinny
Noodles never can taste wrong.

Mother cooked three quarts of squash soup
We ate it cold, we ate it hot
When I went for my tenth helping
There was nothing in the pot.

And so I cooked a box of noodles
I ate a bowl and then some more
My bowl piled high I kept on eating
For clearly noodles I adore.

There's a lesson in here somewhere
What it is I've quite forgot
And so I'll keep on eating noodles
Cold or frozen, warm or hot.

Billy Jo Brown

Billy Jo Brown mixed everything up
He ate his milk with a fork
And drank brown bread from a china cup
Washed clothes with blackboard chalk.

He hoed his yard with a large soup spoon
And slept underneath the car
He wore snow clothes the month of June
Hid his shoes in a jelly jar.

Billy brushed his teeth with a large straw broom
And combed his hair with a rake
Housed nanny goats in the spare guest room
Though their neighing kept him awake.

He whipped sweet cream with a window fan
Then rubbed it in his straight hair,
Bathed Mondays with a watering can
And he never found this queer..

He lay in a boat parked on the grass
In a lightening thunderstorm
Sipping green tea from a demitasse
With claims that it kept him warm.

Billy Jo Brown mixed everything up
Read books held upside down
He ran through town crying "hup! hup! hup!"
And wore feathers for a crown.

Billy Jo Brown—a very good friend
A very good friend indeed
Someone on whom you could depend
Whenever you were in need.

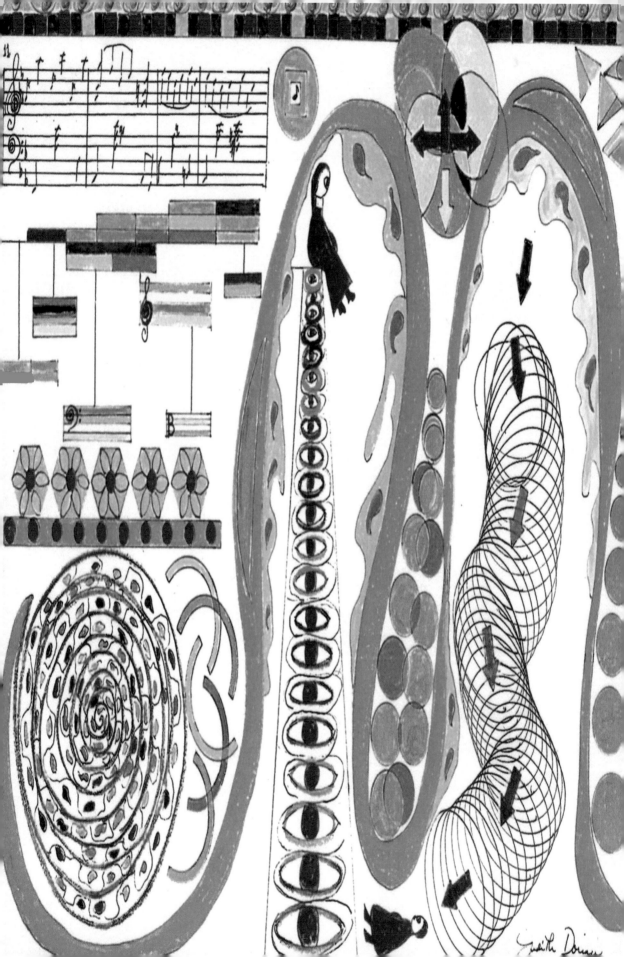

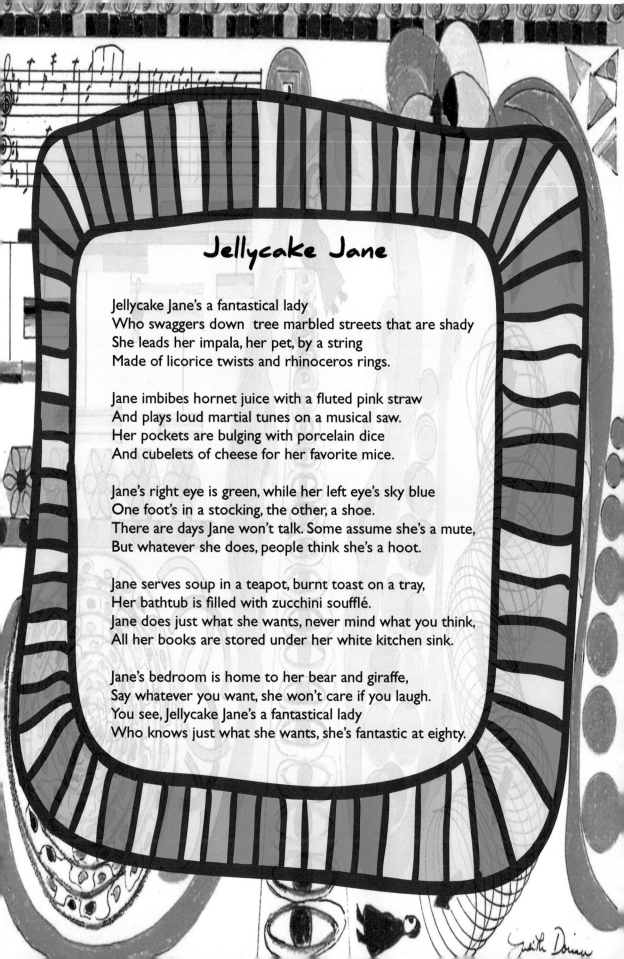

Jellycake Jane

Jellycake Jane's a fantastical lady
Who swaggers down tree marbled streets that are shady
She leads her impala, her pet, by a string
Made of licorice twists and rhinoceros rings.

Jane imbibes hornet juice with a fluted pink straw
And plays loud martial tunes on a musical saw.
Her pockets are bulging with porcelain dice
And cubelets of cheese for her favorite mice.

Jane's right eye is green, while her left eye's sky blue
One foot's in a stocking, the other, a shoe.
There are days Jane won't talk. Some assume she's a mute,
But whatever she does, people think she's a hoot.

Jane serves soup in a teapot, burnt toast on a tray,
Her bathtub is filled with zucchini soufflé.
Jane does just what she wants, never mind what you think,
All her books are stored under her white kitchen sink.

Jane's bedroom is home to her bear and giraffe,
Say whatever you want, she won't care if you laugh.
You see, Jellycake Jane's a fantastical lady
Who knows just what she wants, she's fantastic at eighty.

The Ilegoswitch

Mind ye, never go to the Ilegoswitch
Never even go near, d'ye hear?
You'll be grabbed and twittered and stuck in a ditch
And tossed 40 feet high in the air.

But Johnny won't listen, Johnny does as he wishes
And one night, with the moon full and bright,
Johnny trotted on down to the Ilegoswitch
Tall as an eagle – a dazzling sight.

He danced and he capered and he beat on his drum.
"Come and get me," he cried, "here I am, do your worst
I'm not scared. D'ye hear me? Now come, I say, come
D'ye dare now?" he laughed and laughed—almost to burst.

Then the sky turned bright yellow and chartreuse as the grass,
Lightening lit up the world, the earth shook and rolled.
Thunder rumbled the sky with a terrible blast
And poor Johnny was gone, sucked down deep in the hole.

To this day those brave souls who come close to the site
Say that they hear him still beat on his drum
Hear him laughing and dancing all day and all night
And one brazen young fellow calls, "Come Johnny come."

Mind ye, never go down to the Ilegoswitch
Never even go near, d'ye hear?
You'll be grabbed and twittered and stuck in a ditch
And tossed 40 feet high in the air.

Daybreak

Early in the morning sitting on my window seat
As dawn is coming up I watch the crowd pass on my street.
There's the Gampagoolish lady who is dressed in fur and lace
And Balabushka Mollykle with tattoos on her face.

Behind them trails Kadinki, his pet monkey on a leash,
And rosy Rosadilia with stockinged kalakneesh.
But I always wait for Griggins who belly dances all the way
And Tiggles, his dear partner, with important things to say.

An oolakan comes slithering by, his slimy skin still wet.
And much as I like fish I wouldn't want him as my pet.
And then to my supreme relief, a foogle fangles by
I start to laugh, to giggle, but so hard I finally cry.

And when I think there's no one more, Marushkil comes in sight
Wearing silk pajamas with her pilcher painted white.
She's riding on an ooliplus, her shoes are fuschia leather
Her servant holds a parasol to shade her from the weather.

Then sometimes past the grey schoolyard Papoon, the dink, comes running
To free herself from Sarsparull, the derk who's always punning
But as the sun lights up the street these dear friends go away
With the world returned to ordinary, I start another day.

Pineapple-didouble-dipberry-lope

Come along, come on with me to Daredevil's Hope
I'll buy all the drinks you can drink
A pineapple-didouble-dipberry-lope
Till you find you can no longer think.

One drink will not do it my dear, start with three,
And for safety's sake, sit on a chair.
Sip some raspberry-chocolate-mousse-gator-tail tea
Hold on tight or you'll float through the air.

By the end of the evening, some twenty odd drinks
Will convince you your life is the best
You'll fall into bed catching forty odd winks
You've never had such a good rest.

When you wake in the morning the place won't be there
And you'll find that your hair has turned white
You won't know a soul and you haven't a care
For you'll realize you've turned into light.

Tea Time With Mr. Jack

I have a friend named Mr. Jack
His only friend is me.
We talk of mostly serious things
When he comes here for tea.

He has three pompoms on his hat
And rings on every toe.
When cozying down for a nice chat
His voice is low, so low.

He tells me where the fairies live
And how the mushrooms grow.
There's nothing that I wouldn't give
To know what my friend knows.

He's an encyclopedia,
A living one for sure
Who talks about the habitats
Of unicorns and more.

He's wise about a lot of things—
How rainbows get their color,
How clouds are formed and where they go
In various kinds of weather.

He speaks of other worlds than this
It is his favorite theme
And shows me ways to travel there
To travel through my dreams.

But I have not seen Mr. Jack
At least now for a year
He phoned me from a comet's tail
And soon will reappear.

He's coming back! dear Mr. Jack
And when he does, he'll see
We'll cozy down another time
With a nice cup of tea.

Runaway Vegetables

I went down to my garden patch to plant a row of beans
And heard a voice beside me say "Hi there, I'm Jim McQueen."
"Pleased to meet you sir," I said, looking left and right
"The pleasure's mine," McQueen replied, yet nowhere was in sight.

I placed each seed deep in the ground to comments of McQueen
"It's time to plant tomatoes, for the red looks nice with green."
"There's no room" I cried, then turned, and right before my eyes
A row of red tomatoes stood, each one could win a prize.

"And now you must have yellow," McQueen added with a sigh.
Before I said another word, corn grew up to the sky
"Squash," he said, "and turnip greens, and rutabaga too,
"You must have more, you still don't have enough to make a stew."

McQueen I thought was mad. He didn't understand "enough."
Within an hour a jungle grew whose vines were thick and tough.
Vegetables kept growing. They grew well beyond my yard
They spilled onto the boulevard—caught everyone off guard.

Green peas grew on the highway, while beet tops danced down the lane,
Tall corn blocked city traffic, as squash blossoms went insane.
I dialed 911. "We need help," I cried "and soon."
The city sent a squad equipped with pitchforks and huge spoons.

They couldn't stop the vegetables that blossomed everywhere
As they drove to where the poor folks lived, ill fed and in despair.
Lettuce climbed the broken stairs and tried to get inside.
McQueen, I saw, had a great plan. He clearly was inspired.

"Quick bottle them and freeze them too for winter's on its way
And children will go hungry—we mustn't waste a single day."
Citizens turned out in droves to harvest what they could
Then cleaned, and cooked, and froze and fed the hungry neighborhood.

It took nine months and then a day till order was restored
We all pitched in. Some whined, some laughed, but nobody was bored.
When the streets were clean again a feast was overdue
Together we sat down to eat our vegetable stew.

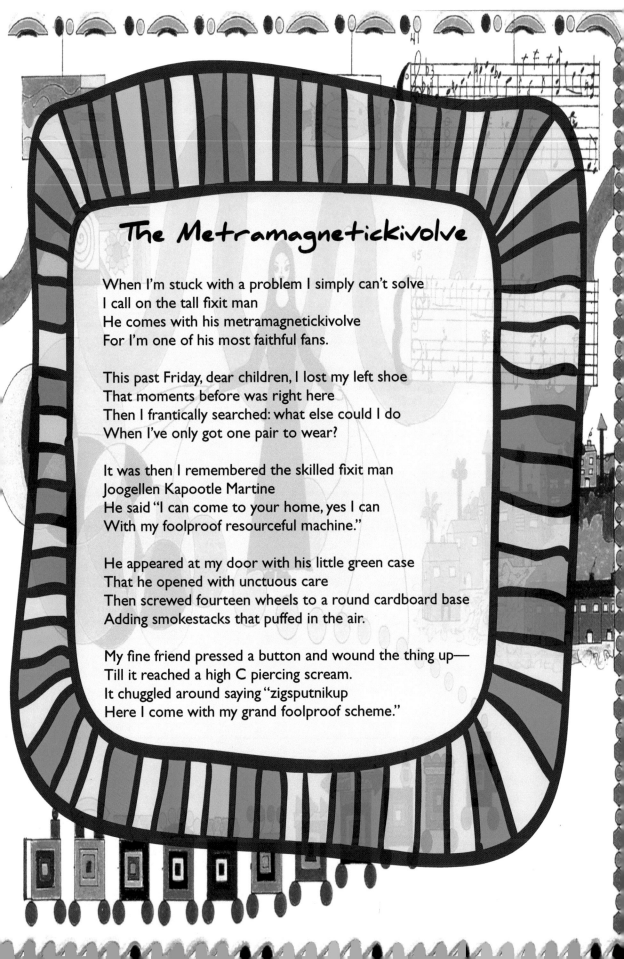

The Metramagnetickivolve

When I'm stuck with a problem I simply can't solve
I call on the tall fixit man
He comes with his metramagnetickivolve
For I'm one of his most faithful fans.

This past Friday, dear children, I lost my left shoe
That moments before was right here
Then I frantically searched: what else could I do
When I've only got one pair to wear?

It was then I remembered the skilled fixit man
Joogellen Kapootle Martine
He said "I can come to your home, yes I can
With my foolproof resourceful machine."

He appeared at my door with his little green case
That he opened with unctuous care
Then screwed fourteen wheels to a round cardboard base
Adding smokestacks that puffed in the air.

My fine friend pressed a button and wound the thing up—
Till it reached a high C piercing scream.
It chuggled around saying "zigsputnikup
Here I come with my grand foolproof scheme."

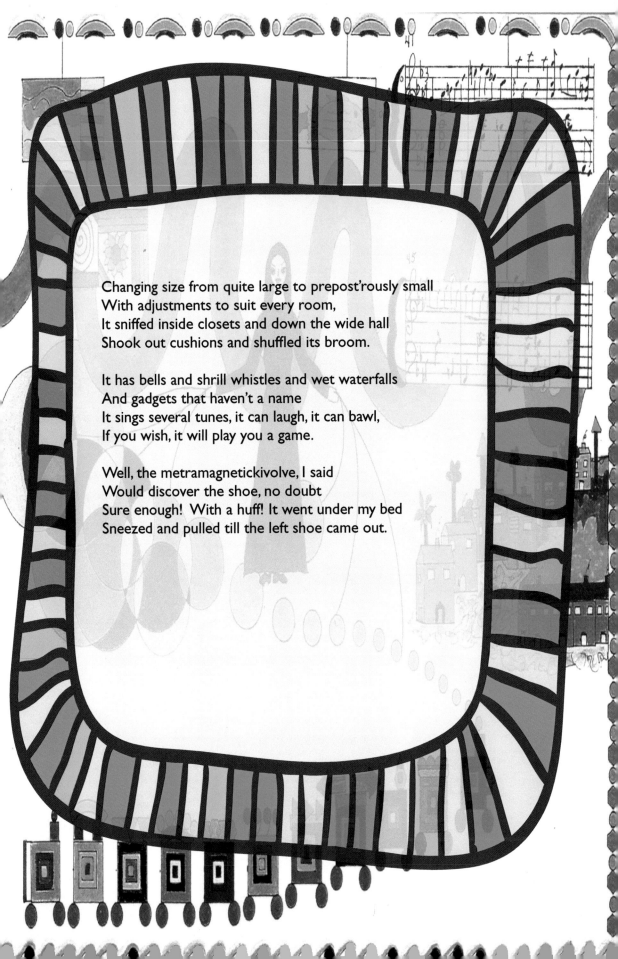

Changing size from quite large to prepost'rously small
With adjustments to suit every room,
It sniffed inside closets and down the wide hall
Shook out cushions and shuffled its broom.

It has bells and shrill whistles and wet waterfalls
And gadgets that haven't a name
It sings several tunes, it can laugh, it can bawl,
If you wish, it will play you a game.

Well, the metramagnetickivolve, I said
Would discover the shoe, no doubt
Sure enough! With a huff! It went under my bed
Sneezed and pulled till the left shoe came out.

Tom Martin MacChase

Do you recall Tom Martin MacChase?
He was our town's hero who won every race.
He had muscles that bulged on his legs and his arms
On his neck, on his torso—all were part of his charm.

As a child Tom could lift ninety pounds in one hand
At a thousand pounds he was named first in the land.
When he lifted 10,000 he caused some alarm
Till a million, a billion could do him no harm.

Tom was swift as the wind as he jumped over stiles.
He swam across rivers—the Tigris, the Nile.
Tom was faster than fast, for hundreds of miles
As he sang in songfests with the swamp crocodiles.

He played ball on your side? Then you never could lose
For the opposite team he would always confuse.
Tom stayed calm, though the crowd stood and roared as he pitched
And the batters struck out; they were clearly bewitched.

Three cheers for our hero Tom Martin MacChase.
I could go on for hours, but I haven't the space.
The truth is I don't have a minute to waste
For I'm trying to catch him, I must leave in all haste.

The Rune of The Killibarigeebee

When the wind comes ripping down the borealic plain
And the ducks in the pond start to loudly complain
You can hear in the distance through the owlish hoot
The bewitching song of a golden lute.

From my bed I rise up in the twilight eerie mist
For I'm drawn by dark songs that I cannot resist
And roll down through the steel grass towards the plaintive tune
Which I know will disclose the ancient rune
Of the Killibarigeebee in the Moreolic land
Etched deep deep down in the shimmering sand.

Darling hold me tight and fold me, bear me on your wings
To the land of wild enchantment and fabuluscious things.
There we'll sing and we'll dance, then we'll pluck the tree-ripe fruit
And live forever in mythic pursuit
Of the Killibarigeebee in the Moreolic land
Etched deep deep down in the shimmering sand.

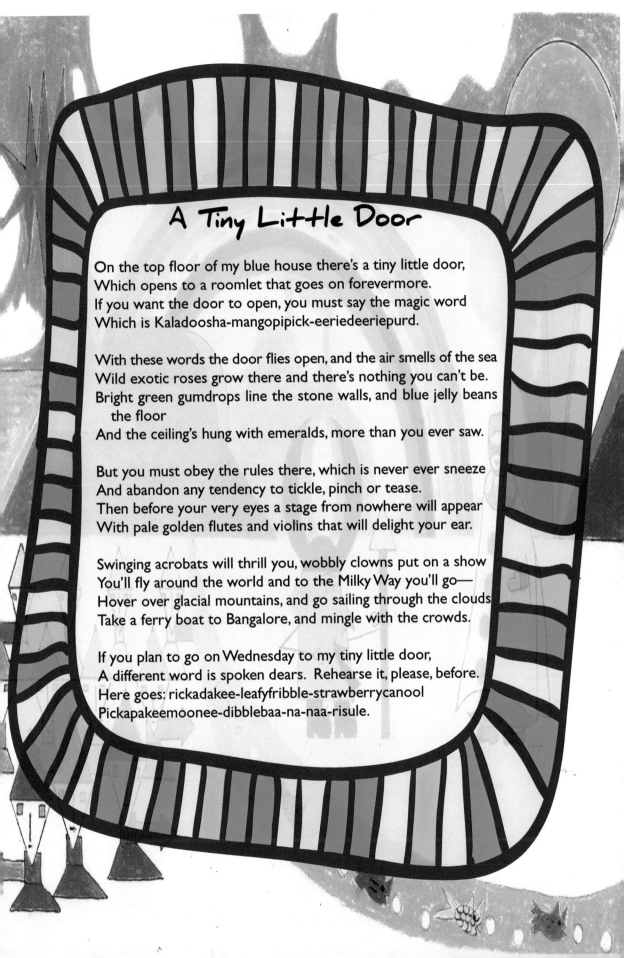

A Tiny Little Door

On the top floor of my blue house there's a tiny little door,
Which opens to a roomlet that goes on forevermore.
If you want the door to open, you must say the magic word
Which is Kaladoosha-mangopipick-eeriedeeriepurd.

With these words the door flies open, and the air smells of the sea
Wild exotic roses grow there and there's nothing you can't be.
Bright green gumdrops line the stone walls, and blue jelly beans
   the floor
And the ceiling's hung with emeralds, more than you ever saw.

But you must obey the rules there, which is never ever sneeze
And abandon any tendency to tickle, pinch or tease.
Then before your very eyes a stage from nowhere will appear
With pale golden flutes and violins that will delight your ear.

Swinging acrobats will thrill you, wobbly clowns put on a show
You'll fly around the world and to the Milky Way you'll go—
Hover over glacial mountains, and go sailing through the clouds
Take a ferry boat to Bangalore, and mingle with the crowds.

If you plan to go on Wednesday to my tiny little door,
A different word is spoken dears. Rehearse it, please, before.
Here goes: rickadakee-leafyfribble-strawberrycanool
Pickapakeemoonee-dibblebaa-na-naa-risule.

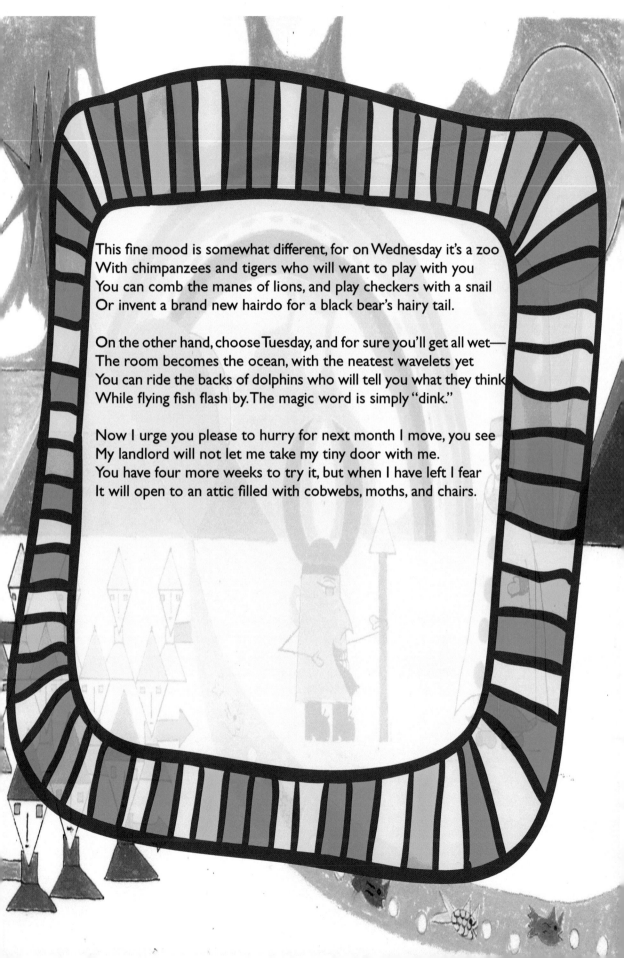

This fine mood is somewhat different, for on Wednesday it's a zoo
With chimpanzees and tigers who will want to play with you
You can comb the manes of lions, and play checkers with a snail
Or invent a brand new hairdo for a black bear's hairy tail.

On the other hand, choose Tuesday, and for sure you'll get all wet—
The room becomes the ocean, with the neatest wavelets yet
You can ride the backs of dolphins who will tell you what they think
While flying fish flash by. The magic word is simply "dink."

Now I urge you please to hurry for next month I move, you see
My landlord will not let me take my tiny door with me.
You have four more weeks to try it, but when I have left I fear
It will open to an attic filled with cobwebs, moths, and chairs.

Friendless

I wonder why nobody loves me
When I'm charming and lovely and bright
People should be delighted to know me
For I'm always unfailingly right.

Why no friends? Well what could be sillier
When I broadcast how splendid I am
My achievements to all are familiar
I'm just grand, super grand, I'll not sham.

And what's more, I'll point out *your* errors
With instruction to better your ways
I'm only too happy to do so
And patient—I'll correct you for days.

Now, to be with, of course, I'm enchanting
But why waste me on myself alone?
In vain I wait for the doorbell
And stare at the so silent phone.

Will You, Won't You?

"Will you speak a little louder?" said the ground hog to the frog.
"What did you say? What say you? I can't hear you in this fog."
"Then I'll come right up beside you and sit down upon your log
I hope you will agree, for I've brought a jug of grog.
Now, will you, won't you, will you, won't you join me in a jog?"

"I should be most delighted," said the frog upon his rug.
"For truth to tell, I'm lonely and I really need a hug.
My children all have left me. Sure, let's dance. I've got the bug.
Let's down that grog, please pour it in this jolly nifty mug.
Now, will you, won't you, will you, won't you give me a big hug?"

So the ground hog and the frog danced upon a lily pad
Until the frog emphatically denied that he was sad.
Then the tadpoles joined the fun and a festival they had.
The fish blew champagne bubbles, most notably the shad.
Now, will you, won't you, won't you please repeat this whole
    ballade?

The Worry Drawer

Whenever I've a worry I just file it in my drawer
Under "W" for worries—I keep adding more and more.
There's the worry for that bully John who beats me after school
And the worry that one day he'll shove and push me in the pool.

Then I worry for each test—will I fail or get an "A"?
And when I meet with strangers will I know just what to say?
Will I always please my parents, will I know how to make friends?
Are my manners really perfect? Do I sometimes give offense?

Will the sky stay high where it belongs, the ocean stocked with fish?
And if I am rewarded will I know just what to wish?
Well, my worries grew to many. They spilled from deep inside
    the drawer.
And before I knew what happened, they all marched outside the door,

I followed in a panic, then I had a great idea
I lit them with a match and watched my problems disappear.
Most worries turned to ashes, though a few went up in smoke
Since that day, I've locked my drawer, so now I'm free to laugh
    and joke.

J. Dorian

Grasshopper Jam

I'm fond of green grasshopper jam
Much valued in old Amsterdam.
But dragonfly pie, I cannot deny
Tingles and stingles me all flim flam.

I'm partial to curried ant soup
That I tasted in far Guadaloupe
Some say that it tickles and eat it with pickles
I think that they're all nincompoops.

Have you ever had butterfly jelly?
It was favored, my dear, by Corelli.
He ate it much hotter—inspiring a cantata
That he wrote for some folks in New Delhi.

Perhaps you've tried bumble bee butter?
Or does the mere thought make you shudder?
I spread it one day on my toast in Bombay
But the bee left and flew to Calcutta.

Some Thoughts on Tootling and Stroogling

When you play on the tootler, it does wondrous things
Drums start to beat and town bells start to ring
Feet start to tap dance and everyone sings
So play on the tootler and ding-a-ling ling.

But do *not* strum the stroogler, you hear me my dear?
The sky will turn black and the sun disappear,
Flowers will wither and mushrooms sprout hair.
So *don't* strum the stroogler and *don't* bring it here.

Yes, play on the tootler, as long as you please,
Then we'll find sugar plums hanging from trees.
And licorice ice cream prepared by queen bees
The tootler, my dear, puts the whole world at ease.

Dining out

I went to the duchess for tea
It was pleasant as pleasant can be
Till in came her pet lamb, put his tail in the jam
And the duchess cried "fiddle-dee-dee".

Invited for lunch with the Pope
I was served an entire cantaloupe
After which we both prayed
Then away I sashayed
And skipped all the way home with a rope.

Dining one day with the king
(Which was deemed by my friends a fine thing)
While eating bean soup, I was seized by the croup
And the servants all started to sing.

At brunch with the bishop one day
His wig moved in a frightening way
When out jumped a gray mouse who ran all
    through the house
To the bishop's enormous dismay.

I went to the home of Duke Luca
Who continually scratched his perruque-a
An ant scuttled out, ran around and about
And began to play on the bazooka.

A Fishy Tale

I have a funny finny fish whom I have nicknamed Jim
Who swishy darts around the tank, then leaps up to its rim.
I planted plankton wild and green, took pebbles blue and pink
And clustered them around the glass. Well then—what do you think?

Jim put each pebble in his mouth, he took them one by one
Then piled them in a chosen spot, he did so just for fun.
Jim scrubbed the pebbles with his fins till each one shone like new
And lined them up, first pinks, then blues; his structure grew and grew.

Now Jim is finicky you see, exact with what he did
At last his bold design emerged—a giant pyramid.
He perched himself upon its point and winked three times at me
I stared astonished at this trick while Jim just laughed with glee.
I wish I understood my fish who seems more like a sprite.
His stunts, his frolic I adore—my Jim, my sheer delight.

The unicorn rarely blows its horn

The unicorn rarely blows its horn
But when it does, beware
For the sound that you hear is so forlorn
It will grip you with grief and fear.

The sound soars high, then falls to low
With a melody that sears your heart
And once it starts it continues to blow
Its awesome eerie art.

The unicorn rarely blows its horn
But when it does, beware
For you heard that sound before you were born
It will always stay in your ears.

How To Swing on A Star

1) Take a roll of white shelving paper, unroll & hang up.
2) Fasten with thumbtacks to the outside of a tall building.
3) Paint stairs onto paper.
4) Wait for the full moon. Put a roll of twine in your pocket and climb up the stairs.
5) On the top stair, tie a lasso. Capture a star and hoist yourself up for the ride of your life.
6) That's all there is to it, although the more adventurous might want to take along a net and connect to a galaxy, swinging from one star to the next.
7) *Word of caution:* don't forget to pack some peanut butter and jelly sandwiches 'cause I don't know the way down.

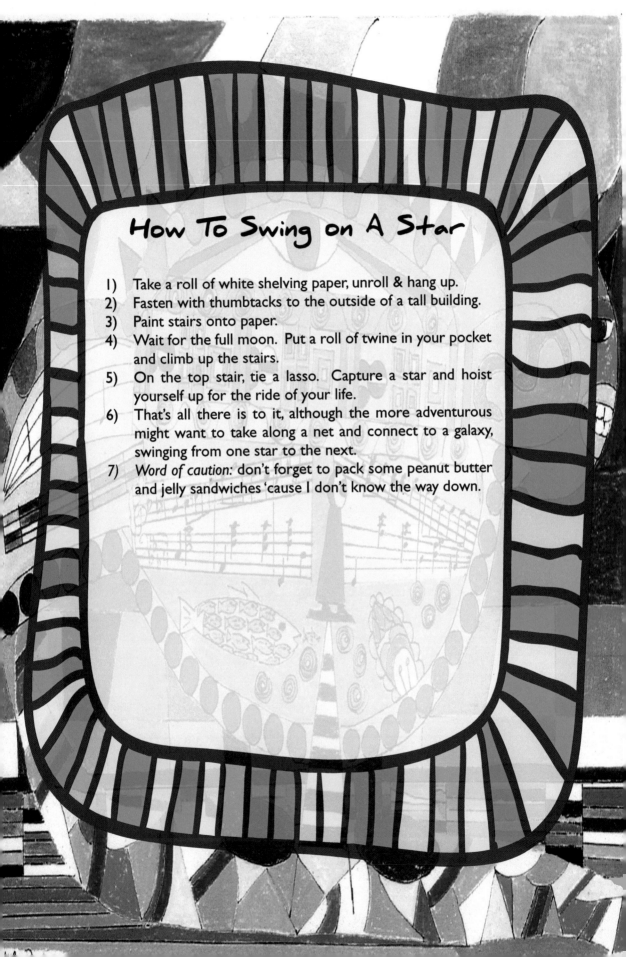

The Muffin Man

Mr. Samuel McMurphy told his wife Charlaine
I'm just about to open up my muffin store
I bought us a shop down on Drury Lane
On Tuesday our first clients can come through the door.
We put blueberry, strawberry, blackberry jam
On our muffins to eat with blue eggs and ham.

Charlaine tenderly embraced her dear husband Sam
And said "why Sam I'll gladly help design the sign
And if you wish I can make several jams."
"Well thank you love," Sam beamed at her. "Why decline?"

So they baked and they cooked and they hung a large sign
A tempting smell of muffins wafted on the air,
The McMurphys sang "We are doing fine"
And were joined by their customer the big Brown Bear.

"I see that our fortune we are going to make,"
Sam hugged his wife and told her with a little laugh
"We will sing all day, you can cook, I shall bake."
"Include me," chimed their client the Blue Giraffe.

Their shop was a success. It became very big.
Sam added one more room--he built it wide and long.
The first to inspect it was Mr. Pig:
"I give it my approval and I give it in song."

The muffin store was famous, it could do no wrong
People poured in by car, by plane and by boat
And all over England you could hear their song
According to the tax collector Mr. Green Goat.
We put blueberry, strawberry, blackberry jam
On our muffins to eat with blue eggs and ham.

Green Velvet Knickers

In green velvet knickers and a green spangled hat
Jerome asked to come in for a warm fireside chat.
We spoke of the weather and the twelve feet of snow.
"Can I stay for the month? I have no place to go."

Jerome likes to whistle ancient tunes through the night
Without pausing for breath until first morning light.
He cooked porridge for breakfast, then swept all the floors,
Chopped wood for the fire, and found ways to do more.

Our friend stayed the month, then remained through late spring
He played ball with our daughter and swung her on swings
Till the woods and the meadows called out to him—then
He knew it was time to get moving again.

He left several years ago—three, perhaps four—
Then this fall when the leaves turned, appeared at our door.
Dressed in green velvet knickers Jerome asked to come in.
He bowed low to the ground, flashed a comical grin.

Our baby was born when we first met Jerome
And didn't know why he was drawn to our home—
He was there for our daughter with eyes of bright green
Who knows things we don't know, has seen things we've not seen.

Alone in the woods she confides in the gnome.
In her sleep she will call out "Jerome, my Jerome!"
So if you have a daughter with shining green eyes
Be observant, be careful, you may be surprised.

Billowing Bubbles

I love to blow billowing bubbles
These I blow the entire day long
And when my friends say there'll be trouble
I start to sing my bubble song.
Bubblee-loo, bubblee- lay. bubblee-tiddlee dei day,
No one can stop me from bubbling today.

On Tuesday I blew one quite monstrous
It flew over trees and the vale
People stared at its size most preposterous
Till it crashed on the nose of a whale.

But my proudest achievement came Wednesday
When the bubble I blew turned out square!
I'd blown that whole week in a frenzy
The result, it is true, of a dare.

Next place on the scale of ambition
Is my plan (I cannot say why)
To lie in a supine position
And blow bubbles some forty feet high.

I'll blow them to Spain and to Turkey
Past morning grass glistening with dew
To Texas and old Albuquerque
For bubbling in Mulligan stew.

You think when they all have alighted
And I've got nothing further to do
Without reason to still be excited
That I'll bid my blue bubbles adieu?

You think so? That thought's full of malice
For faithful I'll always remain
And go to my blue bubble palace
Where I'll sing my blue bubble refrain.
Bubblee-loo, bubblee- lay. bubblee-tiddlee dei day,
No one can stop me from bubbling today.

Commas & Squiggles

Commas & squiggles & others of their ilk
Are lovely to savor with cookies & milk.
Spirals & umlauts & words I can't utter
I've often devoured with omelets & butter.

Colons & brackets [& signs that I fear]
Inspired me to go & wolf down a whole bear!
While notches & crumples & spirals <you see>
Remind me it's time to have crumpets with tea.

Tendrils & whorls, the bold helix & rundles
Call to mind visions of pretzels in bundles.
The crotchet! The hyphen! The breve! The kink!
Please help me prepare some hot chocolate to drink.

The diphthong, the tilde—what a muddle, oh my!
Do cut us three pieces of mulberry pie.
There's so much to know, so much knowledge I lack
What else can I do if not constantly snack?

Quotation marks, arrows, ellipses, the dash
 I'm starving—yes, pass me that crisp corned beef hash
Virgules & shimmies—I'm confused, I admit
I'll eat one more pizza, & then perhaps quit! œ∑´®@#^+_)!!!!!!

Slitheryslamawly and Other Monsters

I like to make up stories
I write them in my head
The best of them are gory
I won't read them before bed.

There's the hairy scary monster
With fangs and bright red eyes
Who hides behind the armchair
And will take you by surprise.

There's the slitheryslamawly
With slimy, oily skin
He'll make you itchycrawly
And kick you in the shins.

And worst, I think, the brastend
Whose tail can fell a tree
And leave you totally flattened
Or crawling on your knees.

But soon my eyes grow tired
I lose control, it seems
I'm no longer inspired
Though who knows what I'll dream?

THE END

CPSIA information can be obtained
at www.ICGtesting.com
Printed in the USA
LVIC031833060112
262757LV00004B